D0255901

Jenny the Pony's New Friends

Jenny the Pony's New Friends

Liz Kessler and Laura Tonge

Illustrated by
Mike Phillips

Orion
Children's Books

First published in Great Britain in 2016
by Orion Children's Books
An imprint of Hachette Children's Books
A division of Hodder and Stoughton Ltd
Carmelite House
50 Victoria Embankment
London EC4Y 0DZ

An Hachette UK Company

1 3 5 7 9 10 8 6 4 2

A catalogue record for this book
is available from the British Library.

ISBN 978 1 4440 1594 2

Printed and bound in China

www.orionchildrensbooks.co.uk

This book is dedicated to the real
Jenny the Pony of Old Mill Stables

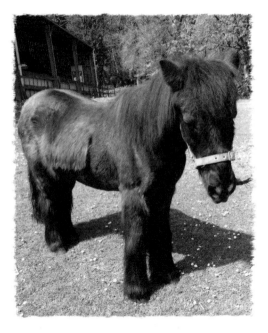

Contents

Chapter One

Jenny stood in her new stable
and watched life go by.

Her owner, Amy, was moving house and Jenny had gone to a new yard. Jenny had to move before Amy, so she would be all on her own for the first week.

'I'll see you in a week,' Amy had said to Jenny. 'Be a good girl and make lots of friends.'

Jenny planned to do exactly that.

A boy who was sweeping
the yard glanced in. 'Hey there,'
he said. 'You're pretty.'

Later, two girls came to take
their ponies for a ride. 'Oh, look,'
one of them said. 'A new pony!
She's so tiny!' They stroked
Jenny's neck and kissed her nose.

'Come on, you two, you'll
be late for your lesson,' a voice
called across the yard, and they
were gone.

Jenny started to feel lonely.
I miss Amy, she thought. No one
had time to be her friend here.

Finally, when the lessons had finished, one of the bigger girls came over to Jenny's stable.

'Hello,' she said. 'My name's Zoe. Your owner says you're the friendliest pony in the world.'

Zoe put a head collar on Jenny. 'You ready to go out in the field?'

Jenny was more than ready to go out to the field. Maybe she'd meet other ponies and make some new friends!

'Have fun,' Zoe said, shutting the gate behind her. 'Someone will come and collect you before night-time.'

Jenny looked around her. No other horses were in this field. How was she ever going to make friends?

Then she noticed a long wooden box at the end of the field. The chicken coop. She had an idea.

Chapter Two

It was almost dark when Jenny heard one of the stable boys, Sam. 'Jenny!' he called. 'Time to come in.'

Jenny didn't come.

'Jenny!' he called more loudly.

Jenny still didn't come.

Finally, Sam spotted Jenny at
the far end of the field, near the
chicken coop. He jumped over the
gate and marched towards her.

But no matter what Sam did,
Jenny wouldn't be caught.

'Please yourself,' Sam said.
'You'll have to sleep out here.'

He shook his head as he headed back to the yard. 'And she was meant to be such a good, friendly girl.'

Jenny felt a bit bad. But when she heard the chickens snoring, she didn't feel too bad.

Next morning, one of the other girls, Sophie, was heading up to the field.

'Watch that new one,' Jenny heard Sam call. 'She's a naughty little thing.'

Sophie led Jenny to her stable.
Peanut was already next door in his.

'Breakfast time,' Sophie said,
tipping hay into Jenny's stable.

Peanut whinnied. 'None for
you, Peanut,' Sophie said. 'You're
on a diet.'

Jenny looked at Peanut. She looked at her hay. Then she remembered what Amy had said about making friends.

Jenny had an idea.

Chapter Three

Later that morning, Marion, the owner of the yard, stopped in front of Jenny's stable. 'Who's made all this mess?' she asked, pointing to a trail of hay spread across the ground.

Sophie was passing. 'Sorry, Marion, I must have spilled it as I was bringing Jenny her breakfast,' she said.

Marion frowned. 'You'd better clean it up. You know I like a tidy yard.'

Jenny felt bad. She knew
Sophie wasn't the one who had
made the mess.

But when Peanut stretched his
neck out to nuzzle against her,
she didn't feel **that** bad.

Lunchtime came around.

As Jenny waited for her food, she heard a squeak. It sounded like a baby's toy being squeezed.

She looked up. Something was bunched in the corner of the roof. A big mound of twigs and leaves – and three tiny beaks!

'Here you go,' Sam said as he put Jenny's food bucket on the floor inside her stable.

Jenny started eating. As soon as Sam was out of sight, she stopped. She looked up again at the hungry babies in the roof. She remembered Amy's words.

Without another thought, Jenny kicked over her bucket. Pony nuts and food spilled everywhere.

She was going to have SO many friends.

When Sam came back, he noticed Jenny's bucket on its side.

'Jenny!' he said. 'Look what you've done!'

Jenny felt bad. But then she heard the squeaky toy sound again and didn't feel too bad.

Chapter Four

That afternoon, the sun went in and it turned cold.

'Rugs on ponies, please,' Marion called.

Sam took one of Jenny's rugs off the shelf in her stable. 'There you go, girl,' he said. 'You'll be nice and warm in this.'

'Has anyone seen Hobnob and Sootie?' Zoe called. Hobnob and Sootie were the stable yard's kittens. They were meant to be rat catchers, but they weren't very good at their job.

Jenny heard a sound in the corner. She looked down and saw two balls of shivering fluff.

Are you cold? Jenny wondered.

Her night-time rug was still folded on the shelf.

She knew what she had to do.

Later, Zoe came to take Jenny out. 'Oh!' she said when she looked inside Jenny's stable. 'How did that happen?'

Jenny's night-time rug was lying in a heap on the floor. Jenny felt a bit bad about that.

Marion walked past as Zoe was leaving Jenny's stable. 'Ah, there you are,' she said to Hobnob and Sootie, who were scurrying across the yard. 'My, my,' she said. 'Wherever you've been hiding, it was certainly somewhere warm.'

Jenny smiled to herself. She didn't feel **that** bad.

Chapter Five

All week, it was the same.

Jenny refused to stay in her stable at night. She would kick at her door until someone took her out.

She dropped hay outside her stable.

She kicked over her food bucket.

She pulled her rug down every afternoon.

When Saturday morning came, Amy arrived with her mum and dad. 'Jenny, I'm here!' she said, throwing her arms round her pony. 'Has she been a good girl?'

'Well,' Zoe said. 'Not exactly. Come with me and I'll show you.'

At breakfast, Amy helped Zoe give Jenny her hay.

Ten minutes later, Jenny's hay was spread all over the ground outside her stable.

'This is what she does every morning!' Zoe said.

Amy pulled Zoe over to the hay bales. 'Crouch down, out of sight,' she said. They watched Jenny pull at her hay and throw it over her door, towards Peanut's stable.

Then they saw Peanut quickly
drag most of it inside his stable
and eat it.

Zoe gasped. 'Peanut is meant
to be on a diet! No wonder he's
gained nearly a kilo this week!'

'Yes, but look what else he's gained,' Amy replied. Peanut had stretched his head right out of his stable and across to Jenny's door. They were nuzzling each other's necks.

Chapter Six

At lunchtime, Amy helped bring
Jenny her food.

As they walked away, they
heard a loud clunk. Jenny
had kicked her bucket over. Zoe
opened her mouth to speak, but
Amy stopped her. 'Look,' she said.

A sparrow flew to the ground and picked up some of the spilled food before flying back up to the roof. She did the same journey over and over.

'Baby sparrows,' Zoe breathed. 'I didn't know we had them.'

Amy smiled. 'Jenny knew,' she said.

In the afternoon, Amy helped put Jenny's rug on.

When they went back twenty minutes later, Jenny had pulled her rug off onto the floor.

'She does this every day!' Zoe said.

Amy noticed something moving inside the rug. She reached down and lifted a corner.

'Hobnob and Sootie!' Zoe said. 'That's where they've been going! We've been worried about them on these frosty days.'

'I don't think you need to worry any more,' Amy said.

As it was getting dark, Jenny
kicked loudly against her stable.

'That's what she does,' Zoe
said. 'She refuses to stay inside
overnight.'

Amy and Zoe took Jenny to her field and followed her up the hill to the chicken coop.

'Ever have any problem with foxes?' Amy asked.

'We've lost six chickens this year. Nothing seems to keep the fox away,' said Zoe.

'Lost any since Jenny came?'
Amy asked.

'Um. No,' said Zoe.

Amy pointed at the door,
where Jenny was standing guard.
'I wonder why.'

'All week, we thought she was
being naughty!' Zoe said.

'She just wants to make friends,'
Amy said.

'Well, she's certainly done that. A pony, two kittens, a mummy bird and her three babies and fifteen chickens. I think she deserves an award!'

'Why not give her one, then?' Amy asked.

Zoe smiled. 'Maybe we can.'

Chapter Seven

Next morning, everyone gathered
by Jenny's stable.

'We're giving out a special award today,' Marion said. She reached into her pocket and brought out a shiny gold rosette with a big number ONE on it. 'I would like to award the prize for friendliest pony in the world to . . . Jenny!'

Jenny couldn't believe what she was hearing. She'd won an award!

Amy pinned Jenny's rosette on her head collar.

I'm the friendliest pony in the world, Jenny thought to herself proudly.

And later that day, as Peanut nibbled on his hay, Hobnob and Sootie snuggled up in their cosy bed, three baby birds had full tummies and fifteen chickens slept soundly, it was clear that everyone agreed.